Raggs Prese

The 45 Presidents

Enjoy the "The 45 Presidents" song and music video!

Written by Toni Steedman Zelickson
Coordination by Alexandra Anderson

Art Direction by Dabney Estile
Lead Illustrator Jeff Mangum

 ISBN 978-0-692-80162-8

THE 45 PRESIDENTS QUICK REFERENCE

#	President	Party	Term	Wives and Spouses
1	George Washington	Nonpartisan	1789-1797	Martha Washington
2	John Adams	Federalist	1797-1801	Abigail Adams
3	Thomas Jefferson	Democratic-Republican	1801-1809	Martha Jefferson
4	James Madison	Democratic-Republican	1809-1817	Dolley Madison
5	James Monroe	Democratic-Republican	1817-1825	Elizabeth Monroe
6	John Quincy Adams	Democratic-Republican	1825-1829	Louisa Catherine Adams
7	Andrew Jackson	Democratic	1829-1837	Rachel Jackson
8	Martin Van Buren	Democratic	1837-1841	Hannah Van Buren
9	William Henry Harrison	Whig	1841-1841	Anna Harrison
10	John Tyler	Whig	1841-1845	Letitia Tyler/Julia Tyler
11	James K. Polk	Democratic	1845-1849	Sarah Polk
12	Zachary Taylor	Whig	1849-1850	Margaret "Peggy" Taylor
13	Millard Fillmore	Whig	1850-1853	Abigail Fillmore/ Caroline Fillmore
14	Franklin Pierce	Democratic	1853-1857	Jane Pierce
15	James Buchanan	Democratic	1857-1861	(Never married)
16	Abraham Lincoln	Republican	1861-1865	Mary Todd Lincoln
17	Andrew Johnson	National Union	1865-1869	Eliza Johnson
18	Ulysses S. Grant	Republican	1869-1877	Julia Grant
19	Rutherford B. Hayes	Republican	1877-1881	Lucy Hayes
20	James A. Garfield	Republican	1881-1881	Lucretia Garfield
21	Chester A. Arthur	Republican	1881-1885	Ellen Arthur

22	Grover Cleveland	Democratic	1885-1889	Frances Cleveland
23	Benjamin Harrison	Republican	1889-1893	Caroline Harrison/ Mary Scott Harrison
24	Grover Cleveland	Democratic	1893-1897	Frances Cleveland
25	William McKinley	Republican	1897-1901	Ida McKinley
26	Theodore Roosevelt	Republican	1901-1909	Alice Lee Roosevelt/ Edith Roosevelt
27	William H. Taft	Republican	1909-1913	Helen "Nellie" Taft
28	Woodrow Wilson	Democratic	1913-1921	Ellen Wilson/Edith Wilson
29	Warren G. Harding	Republican	1921-1923	Florence Harding
30	Calvin Coolidge	Republican	1923-1929	Grace Coolidge
31	Herbert Hoover	Republican	1929-1933	Lou Hoover
32	Franklin D. Roosevelt	Democratic	1933-1945	Eleanor Roosevelt
33	Harry S. Truman	Democratic	1945-1953	Elizabeth "Bess" Truman
34	Dwight D. Eisenhower	Republican	1953-1961	Mamie Eisenhower
35	John F. Kennedy	Democratic	1961-1963	Jacqueline "Jackie" Kennedy
36	Lyndon B. Johnson	Democratic	1963-1969	Claudia "Lady Bird" Johnson
37	Richard M. Nixon	Republican	1969-1974	Thelma "Pat" Nixon
38	Gerald R. Ford	Republican	1974-1977	Elizabeth Ann "Betty" Ford
39	James E. Carter Jr.	Democratic	1977-1981	Eleanor "Rosalynn" Carter
40	Ronald Reagan	Republican	1981-1989	Jane Wyman/Nancy Reagan
41	George H.W. Bush	Republican	1989-1993	Barbara Bush
42	William Jefferson Clinton	Democratic	1993-2001	Hillary Rodham Clinton
43	George W. Bush	Republican	2001-2009	Laura Bush
44	Barack H. Obama	Democratic	2009-2017	Michelle Obama
45	Donald John Trump Sr.	Republican	2017-	Ivana Trump/Marla Maples/ Melania Trump

Create Your Own Flag

"OLD GLORY"

Our Flag's Nickname

Our country's first official flag since June 14, 1777.

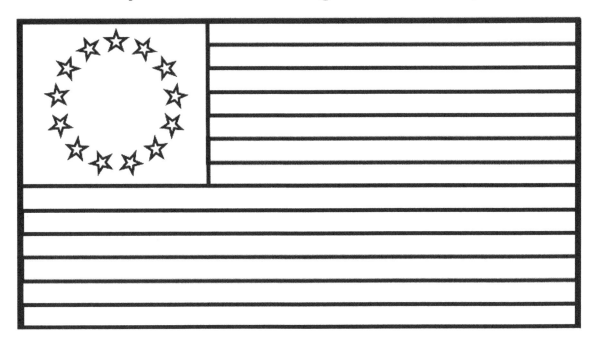

The flag today since July 4, 1960.

The Washington Monument

The Washington Monument was completed and
opened to the public in 1888.

George
WASHINGTON

Presidency:	April 30, 1789 – March 4, 1797
Nickname:	"Father of our Country"
Occupations:	Surveyor, Farmer, Commander of the Continental Army
History:	Organized the first government and kept the states unified.
Home:	Mt. Vernon, Virginia (open to visit)

Abigail Adams

Wife of John Adams, the second president; advisor to her husband; advocated women's rights; wrote over 1,000 letters to her husband while he was away.

John
ADAMS

Presidency: March 4, 1797 – March 4, 1801

Occupations: Lawyer, foreign diplomat, Vice President to Washington

History: One of five people who authored the Declaration of Independence; had the complicated job of building the new country and keeping peace.

Home: He and his wife, Abigail, were the first to occupy The White House.

Declaration of Independence Preamble

Fill in the blanks with the correct words below:

happiness   green   rights   wrong   liberty   juice   bacon   life   party

equal   lies   truths   clues   honest   flying saucers   moons   chocolate

We hold these_____to be

self-evident, that all men are created _____,

that they are endowed, by their Creator, with certain

unalienable _____that among these are

_____, _____, and the

pursuit of _____.

Answers: Page 84

Thomas
JEFFERSON

Presidency: March 4, 1801 – March 4, 1809

Occupations: Author, philosopher, musician, inventor, farmer, lawyer, architect, foreign diplomat, Vice President to Adams

History: Wrote the first draft of the Declaration of Independence; negotiated Louisiana Purchase from France; sent Lewis & Clark on a famous expedition.

Home: Monticello, near Charlottesville, VA (open to visit)

James
MADISON

Presidency: March 4, 1809 – March 4, 1817

Occupation: Government service

History: Helped to write the U.S. Constitution, especially the "Bill of Rights;" peace treaty to end the War of 1812.

Fun Fact: During the war, the British burned The White House and, Madison's wife, Dolley, had to flee to the woods. According to legend, she saved the original copy of the Declaration of Independence!

James
MONROE

Presidency: March 4, 1817 – March 4, 1825

Occupations: Revolutionary war soldier, lawyer

History: One of the Founding Fathers; Established Monroe Doctrine to protect North & South America from invasion; Missouri Compromise; bought Florida from Spain.

Fun Fact: He and his wife attended Napoleon I's Coronation at Notre Dame Cathedral in France.

John Quincy
ADAMS

Presidency: March 4, 1825 – March 4, 1829

Occupations: Lawyer, foreign diplomat, professor, foreign ambassador, congressman, Secretary of State

History: Son of President #2, John Adams; opposed slavery; purchased Florida; drafted the Monroe Doctrine.

Fun Fact: Kept a diary for most of his life – a total of 14,000 pages!

Andrew
JACKSON

Presidency:	March 4, 1829 – March 4, 1837
Nickname:	"Old Hickory"
Occupations:	Soldier, farmer, statesman
History:	First president born in the South, near Waxhaw, NC; supported slavery; responsible for displacing American Indian tribes known as the "Trail of Tears."
Fun Fact:	Opened The White House to the public for his wild inauguration party.

15

Myth Buster

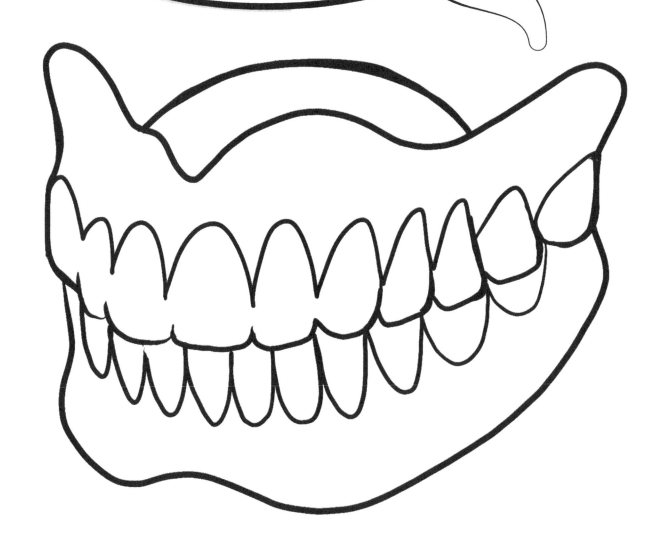

George Washington's teeth weren't made of wood! They were made of animal teeth, ivory and human teeth.

Martin
VAN BUREN

Presidency: March 4, 1837 – March 4, 1841

Occupations: Lawyer, politician, Vice President to Jackson

History: Inherited banking crisis called Panic of 1837.

Fun Fact: Known for "cutting through red tape" to get things done!

Dolley Madison

Popular First Lady, influential hostess and fashionista. Dolley made the turban popular!

Sarah Angelica Singleton Van Buren

Daughter-in-Law to Martin Van Buren and official First Lady during his administration because his wife had died many years before.

William Henry
HARRISON

Presidency: March 4, 1841 – April 4, 1841

Nickname: "Tippecanoe," won Battle of Tippecanoe against American Indians

Occupations: American military officer, politician, attended medical school

History: Died of pneumonia after 32 days in office, shortest term of any president.

Fun Fact: Grandfather of Benjamin Harrison, President #23

John
TYLER

Presidency: April 4, 1841 – March 4, 1845
Occupations: Lawyer, politician, Vice President to Harrison
History: Succeeded Harrison upon his death; helped to annex Texas; sided with South in Civil War.
Fun Fact: Had fifteen children!

White House Pets

Which president had a pet alligator and kept him in the East Room bathtub?

– – – –   – – – –   – – – –

Answer: Page 84

White House Pets

Which president had a small zoo at The White House
that included a famous pygmy hippo named "Billy?"

_ _ _ _ _ _ 　 _ _ _ _ _ _ _

Answer: Page 84

James K. POLK

Presidency: March 4, 1845 – March 4, 1849

Occupations: Lawyer, politician, farmer

History: Reduced tariffs; settled borders with Canada and Mexico leading to the new states of Oregon, Washington, California, Arizona, Nevada, Utah and New Mexico.

Fun Fact: Worked 12-16 hours/day and no vacations! Issued first postage stamp.

Zachary
TAYLOR

Presidency: March 4, 1849 – July 9, 1850

Occupations: War hero of four wars - War of 1812, Black Hawk War, Seminole War, Mexican War

History: California Gold Rush; died a little over a year into presidency.

Fun Fact: Kept his horse, Old Whitey, on the White House lawn.

White House Pets

Who was the last cow to live at The White House?

Clue: She belonged to President Taft.

_ _ _ _ _ _ _

Answer: Page 84

White House Pets

Which president kept sheep to mow The White House lawn?

_ _ _ _ _ _ _   _ _ _ _ _

Answer: Page 84

13

Millard
FILLMORE

Presidency:	July 9, 1850 – March 4, 1853
Occupations:	Textile apprentice, lawyer, politician, Vice President to Taylor
History:	Succeeded Taylor upon his death; tried to find compromise for slave and non-slave states called the Compromise of 1850.
Fun Fact:	Little education until age nineteen and future wife, Abigail, was his teacher.

Franklin
PIERCE

Presidency: March 4, 1853 – March 4, 1857

Occupations: Lawyer, soldier, politician

History: Kansas-Nebraska Bill was created; aquired addtional land from Mexico and launched discussions to acquire Alaska from Russia.

Fun Fact: He was the first President to present his address from memory - all 3,000 words!

James
BUCHANAN

Presidency: March 4, 1857 – March 4, 1861

Occupations: Lawyer, politician

History: Proslavery; Dred Scott case and John Brown battle in Harper's Ferry, VA.

Fun Fact: Only president who never married.

Find combinations of bills that will equal the total.

(Hint: There are many combinations.)

_____ + _____ + _____ = $25.00

$1 bill $2 bill $5 bill

_____ + _____ + _____ = $157.00

$1 bill $2 bill $5 bill

_____ + _____ + _____ = $926.00

$1 bill $2 bill $5 bill

Gettysburg Address

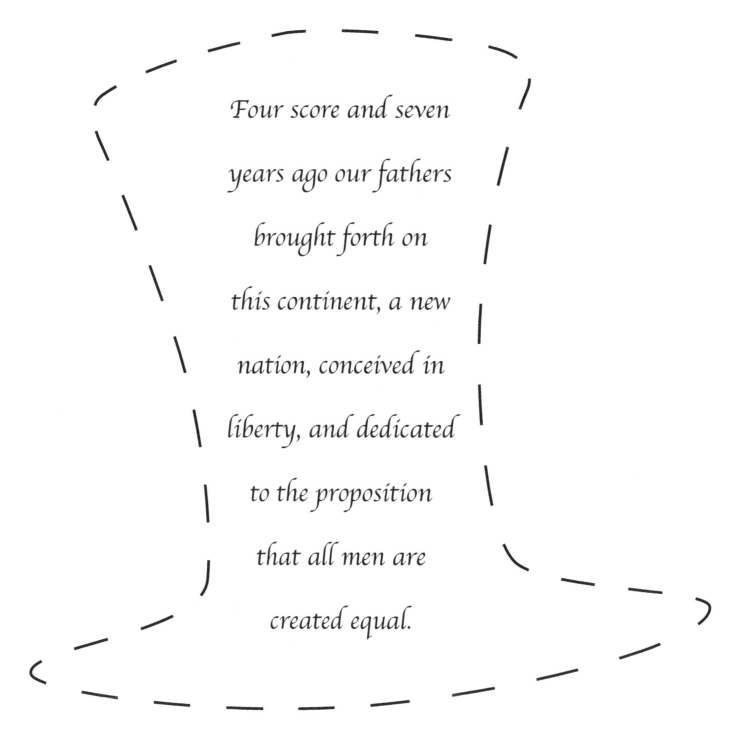

Four score and seven years ago our fathers brought forth on this continent, a new nation, conceived in liberty, and dedicated to the proposition that all men are created equal.

President Lincoln delivered the *Gettysburg Address* at the Dedication of the Cemetery at Gettysburg, PA on November 19, 1863. Above is the opening sentence of a very short (272 words), but powerful speech.

Abraham
LINCOLN

Presidency: March 4, 1861 – April 15, 1865

Nickname: "Honest Abe"

Occupations: Postmaster, lawyer, farmer, politician

History: Wrote the *Emancipation Proclamation* to end slavery; held the country together during the Civil War; assassinated by John Wilkes Booth at Ford's Theatre.

Fun Fact: Honored in the Wrestling Hall of Fame, defeated only once in over 300 matches!

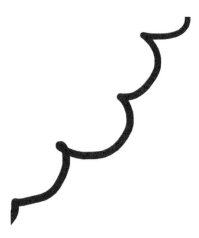

The White House

FUN FACTS:

Address: 1600 Pennsylvania Avenue NW
                Washington, DC 20500

Home to U.S. presidents since 1800.

132 rooms, 35 bathrooms, 6 floors totaling 55,000 sq. ft.

Includes a tennis court, jogging track, swimming pool, theater, billiard room and bowling lane.

17

Andrew
JOHNSON

Presidency: April 5, 1865 – March 4, 1869

Occupations: Tailor, politician, Vice President to Lincoln

History: Became president when Lincoln was assassinated; inherited problems of how to treat newly freed slaves and reconstruction of the country after the Civil War.

Fun Fact: Since he was a tailor, Johnson wore suits he made himself!

Ulysses S.
GRANT

Presidency: March 4, 1869 – March 4, 1877

Occupations: Soldier, farmer, shopkeeper, U.S. Army General

History: Lead the Union army during the American Civil War; Civil Rights Acts of 1870 & 1875 guaranteeing equal rights to African-Americans.

Fun Facts: Grant's favorite horse was named Cincinnati, the son of one of the fastest horses in the U.S. at that time. In most statues, Grant is astride Cincinnati.

19

Rutherford B. HAYES

Presidency: March 4, 1877 – March 4, 1881

Occupations: Lawyer, soldier, politician

History: Didn't win the popular vote or Electoral College – Congress had to decide; worked hard to heal the nation after the Civil War; consulted with Frederick Douglass, the renowned African American leader.

Fun Fact: His wife, Lucy, was the first First Lady to attend college. She also started The White House Easter Egg Roll traditional event.

James A. GARFIELD

Presidency: March 4, 1881 – September 19, 1881

Occupations: Lawyer, teacher, preacher, janitor, carpenter, soldier, U.S. Army general, congressman

History: Assassinated after 11 months; tried to stop political "patronage," giving jobs to friends and supporters.

Fun Fact: Worked as a janitor to help pay for college.

Chester A.
ARTHUR

Presidency: September 19, 1881 – March 4, 1885

Occupations: Teacher, lawyer, tax collector, politician, Vice President to Garfield

History: Became president after Garfield's assassination; signed the Pendleton Civil Service Reform Act, required government workers to test for job qualification; enhanced the strength of the U.S. Navy with new steam-powered engines.

Fun Fact: Loved to dress well, owned 80 pairs of pants!

Who was the tallest president at 6' 4"?

James Madison was the shortest at 5'3".

William Howard Taft was the heaviest at 340 lbs.

(Although he went on several diets and eventually better controlled his weight.)

Answer: Page 84

Grover
CLEVELAND

Presidency: March 4, 1885 – March 4, 1889
March 4, 1893 – March 4, 1897

Occupations: Sheriff, lawyer, politician

History: Only president to serve two non-consecutive terms; vetoed twice as many bills as all 21 previous presidents combined; had to deal with The Panic of 1893, worst financial crisis in country to date.

Fun Fact: Married Frances Folsom, who was 21 and youngest First Lady in history, at The White House .

Benjamin
HARRISON

Presidency: March 4, 1889 – March 4, 1893

Occupations: Lawyer, soldier, journalist, politician

History: Country was growing and decisions were more complex; signed Sherman Anti-Trust Act, and the Sherman Silver Purchase Act.

Fun Fact: His grandfather was William Henry Harrison, President #9.

Air Force One

Fun Facts:

There are 2 identical Air Force One planes (one is always available).

Air Force One can be refueled in the air.

It features 4,000 square feet of space includes presidential quarters, meeting rooms, a chef's kitchen, gym and medical rooms.

The President's limousine (car) travels on Air Force One.

William
MCKINLEY

Presidency:	March 4, 1897 – September 14, 1901
Occupations:	Soldier, lawyer, politician
History:	U.S. became a true world power by fighting Spanish to help Cuba; became the third assassinated president.
Fun Fact:	First president to ride in a car.

Presidential Speech Practice

Fill in the blanks below, then place the words in the speech.

1. Vegetable_____

2. Animal_____

3. Candy or toy_____

4. Friend's name_____

5. Number_____

6. Number_____

7. Sport or Activity_____

8. Number_____

9. Name of person, pet or country_____

As President, I promise to lead by example.

I will eat all the (1)_____on my plate, take care

of my (2)_____, and share my

(3)_____with my friend

(4)_____.

I promise to bathe every (5)_____ days and

brush my teeth (6)_____ times a day.

I will and give 100% at (7)_____.

I promise to read at least (8)_____

books per week.

I promise to be nicer to (9)_____.

26

Theodore
ROOSEVELT

Presidency: September 14, 1901 – March 4, 1909

Occupations: Rancher, soldier, politician, Vice President to McKinley

History: Became president when McKinley was assassinated; built the Panama Canal, introduced the "Square Deal" to make food and drugs safer; a great outdoorsman who created the U.S. Forest Service.

Fun Fact: Read books every day, wrote more than 35 books and 150,000 letters.

Because Theodore Roosevelt refused to shoot a bear cub on a hunting trip, stuffed bears were soon called _ _ _ _ _ bears!

Answer: page 84

27

William H.
TAFT

Presidency: March 4, 1909 – March 4, 1913

Occupations: Lawyer, judge, dean of law school, Secretary of War, Supreme Court Chief Justice

History: Worked to break up trusts and monopolies; established a parcel post service; signed the Sixteenth Amendment creating the federal income tax.

Fun Fact: Heaviest president at 340 lbs; had a giant bathtub. (Eventually, he better controlled his weight.)

Woodrow
WILSON

Presidency: March 4, 1913 – March 4, 1921

Occupations: Lawyer, professor, university president, politician, Governor of New Jersey

History: Tried to keep us out of World War I, but in 1917 he declared war and the U.S. joined the Allies. After the war ended in 1918, Wilson tried to organize peace-keeping nations into the League of Nations. Wilson signed the 19th Amendment giving women the right to vote!

Fun Facts: Wilson was famous for being really smart even though he had dyslexia, a learning difference that makes it difficult to read.

Who Said It?

Match the quote with the President who said it.

"The only thing we have to fear is fear itself!"

"Ask not what your country can do for you; ask what you can do for your country!"

"Mr. Gorbachev, open this gate! Mr. Gorbachev, tear down this wall!"

"Speak softly, and carry a big stick."

"I pray Heaven to bestow the best of blessings on this house (The White House) and all that shall hereafter inhabit it. May none but honest and wise men ever rule under this roof."

Answers: Page 84

29

Warren G.
HARDING

Presidency: March 4, 1921 – August 2, 1923

Occupations: Newspaper editor & publisher, Senator from Ohio

History: His administration was known for corruption, but he also helped the country get back on track after WWI by lowering taxes and helping businesses grow. He died while in office.

Fun Fact: Loved to gamble and lost The White House china in a poker game.

Calvin
COOLIDGE

Presidency: August 2, 1923 – March 4, 1929

Occupations: Lawyer, politician, Vice President to Harding

History: Became president when Harding died; lowered taxes; signed the Indian Citizen Act, giving citizenship to all American Indians.

Fun Facts: He was sworn in as President by his father, a justice of the peace.

Herbert
HOOVER

Presidency: March 4, 1929 – March 4, 1933

Occupations: Gold miner, geologist, engineer, businessman, politician, Secretary of Commerce

History: Popular president who worked hard, but could not find a quick solution to the Great Depression; enacted good programs for children, prison reform and expanded national parks.

Fun Fact: Hoover Dam named after him; was nominated five times for the Nobel Peace Prize.

Match the First Ladies with Their Husbands.

Sarah

Martha

Eleanor

Dolley

Abigail

President
F. D. Roosevelt

President
Fillmore

President
Washington

President
Polk

President
Madison

Match the First Ladies with Their Husbands.

 Laura

 President Kennedy

 Lady Bird

 President Ford

 Jackie

 President G. W. Bush

 Rosalynn

 President Johnson

 Betty

 President Carter

Franklin D.
ROOSEVELT

Presidency: March 4, 1933 – April 12, 1945

Nickname: "FDR"

Occupations: Lawyer, politician, Governor of New York

History: Initiated the "New Deal" to pull the country out of the Great Depression; engaged the U.S. in WWII when Japan attacked Pearl Harbor; served 12 years, longest of any president; died just before the end of WWII while still in office.

Fun Fact: Contracted polio at age 39, paralyzing his legs, but he did not let this disability stop him!

33

Harry S. TRUMAN

Presidency:	April 12, 1945 – January 20, 1953
Occupations:	Railroad worker, farmer, retailer, senator, Vice President to Roosevelt
History:	Had to make the historic decision to use atomic bomb to end WWII; worked to improve lives of everyday people and people affected by the war.
Fun Fact:	Met his wife, "Bess," in Sunday School at 6 years old!

Dwight D.
EISENHOWER

Presidency: January 20, 1953 – January 20, 1961

NIckname: "Ike"

Occupations: Soldier, Five-star U.S. Army General

History: Worked to keep peace during "Cold War" with Russia and ended the Korean War; sponsored and signed the Civil Rights Bill of 1957 and the act to build our interstate highway system.

Fun Facts: Was superstitious and carried three lucky coins in his pocket!

Jacqueline "Jackie" Kennedy

Famous and stylish wife of JFK. She was a patron of the arts who oversaw restoration of The White House and worked to help restore Lafayette Square in Washington, D.C., and New York City's Grand Central Terminal.

John F.
KENNEDY

Presidency: January 20, 1961 – November 20, 1963

Nickname: "JFK"

Occupations: Author, U.S. Navy sailor, Senator from Massachusetts

History: War hero who later avoided war with Russia over missiles in Cuba; created the Peace Corps; assassinated in Dallas, TX parade.

Fun Fact: His presidency was often referred to as "Camelot," one of Kennedy's favorite plays and a reference to a happier time.

Lyndon B.
JOHNSON

Presidency: November 22, 1963 – January 20, 1969

Occupations: Teacher, politician, Vice President to Kennedy

History: Succeeded Kennedy after assassination; enacted many of Kennedy's ideas and many of his own including Medicare, Medicaid, Head Start program and food stamps; sent troops to the controversial Vietnam War. (There were many protests in U.S. against the war.)

Fun Fact: His nickname was "LBJ" and his wife and daughters also had the same initials!

Richard M.
NIXON

Presidency: January 20, 1969 – August 9, 1974

Occupations: Lawyer, U.S. Navy sailor, politician

History: Nixon administration accomplishments include   landing the first American on the moon, ending the Vietnam War and enacting new environmental laws, but due to the "Watergate" scandal Nixon was the first president to resign from office.

Fun Facts: Nixon wasn't known to be a funny guy, but his appearance on the *Laugh In* TV show helped him get elected!

Mount Rushmore

Mount Rushmore Word Scramble

It took 14 years, 1927 -1941, to sculpt the heads of four presidents into the solid granite face of Mount Rushmore, located in the Black Hills in Keystone, South Dakota.

_ _ _ _ _ _ _ _ _ _

I N G A S H W N O T

_ _ _ _ _ _ _ _ _

S O N F J E F E R

_ _ _ _ _ _ _ _ _

T E L O O R E V S

_ _ _ _ _ _ _

C O L N L N I

Answers: Page 84

Gerald R.
FORD

Presidency: August 9, 1944 – January 20, 1977

Occupations: Male model, U. S. Navy sailor, lawyer, politician

History: Succeeded Nixon after resignation and pardoned him; presided over worst economy since the Great Depression.

Fun Fact: Star football player at the University of Michigan, but was known to be a clumsy president!

James E.
CARTER JR.

Presidency: January 20, 1977 – January 20, 1981

Occupations: U.S. Navy sailor, peanut farmer, writer, politician, Governor of Georgia, activitist

History: Helped Israel and Egypt sign a famous peace treaty.

Fun Facts: Won the Nobel Peace prize for his good works after leaving office, especially his support of Habitat for Humanity, where he helped build affordable houses.

Ronald
REAGAN

Presidency: January 20, 1981 – January 20, 1989

Nickname: "Dutch" and "Gipper"

Occupations: Actor, broadcaster, president of the Screen Actors Guild, Governor of California

History: Lowered taxes to encourage economic growth; built a strong military and helped to end the "Cold War" with Russia; helped bring down the Berlin Wall that split Germany.

Fun Fact: He was a famous actor and his wife, Nancy, was once a famous actress!

Color & Count President Reagan's Jelly Beans!

Answer: Page 84

To help him quit smoking a pipe, President Reagan started snacking on jelly beans and ordered 306,070 beans per month to be distributed to The White House, Capitol Hill and federal buildings!

Republican Elephant

Democratic Donkey

41

George H. W.
BUSH

Presidency: January 20, 1989 – January 20, 1993

Occupations: U.S. Navy pilot, businessman, Director of the CIA, ambassador, Vice President to Reagan

History: Raised taxes because the government was losing money; assembled an army of soldiers from more than 30 nations to help defeat Saddam Hussein in the Gulf War.

Fun Fact: His plane was shot down in WWII and he parachuted to safety then celebrated his 80th, 85th and 90th birthdays with parachute jumps!

42

William Jefferson
CLINTON

Presidency: January 20, 1993 – January 20, 2001

Occupations: Lawyer, law professor, Governor of Arkansas

History: Popular president during a period of strong economic growth; even worked with the opposing party, Republicans, to balance the U.S. budget.

Fun Facts: Loved to play the saxophone and even played at his own inaugural ball!

Freedom Tower

September 11, 2001, is one of the saddest days in American history. Terrorists attacked the twin towers of the World Trade Center in New York City and the Pentagon in Washington, DC, and attempted to attack The White House. On the site of the original towers now stands the Freedom Tower. At the base of the Freedom tower are two large reflecting pools commemorating those who lost their lives on 9/11.

George W.
BUSH

Presidency: January 20, 2001 – January 20, 2009

Occupations: Businessman, baseball team owner, Governor of Texas

History: After 9/11 attack, he declared the "War on Terrorism;" initiated multiple efforts including the invasion of Iraq; major financial crisis at end of term.

Fun Fact: Won the election with more electoral votes, but the other candidate, Al Gore, had 543,895 more popular votes!

Let's Move

Michelle Obama's program to raise a healthier generation.

What did Michelle grow in
The White House garden?
Circle all that apply.

sea kale	cabbage
carrots	rice
spinach	lavender
Lincoln oats	corn
spearmint	pumpkins
garlic	lemon grass
fennel	peanuts
tomatillos	milkweed
shallots	figs
endive	onions
brussels sprouts	

Answer: Page 84

Barack H.
OBAMA

Presidency: January 20, 2009 – January 20, 2017

Occupations: Activist, lawyer, law professor, U.S. Senator from Illinois

History: First African American president; used government "Bail Out" program to end the recession; passed affordable health care law; brought troops back from the Middle East and ordered the mission that killed Osama bin Laden, the terrorist leader responsible for 9/11.

Fun Fact: He promised his daughters, Malia and Natasha, a dog if he won the presidency. Two Portuguese water dogs, Bo and Sunny, joined the family!

Today's Presidential Seal

The Presidential Seal is the official symbol of the office of the President of the United States. It includes the President's coat of arms, an eagle on the great seal, a ring of stars and the words, Seal of the President of the United States.

Donald John
TRUMP SR.

Presidency: January 20, 2017 –

Occupations: Businessman, entrepreneur, author, reality TV host, politician

History: Real estate developer who conceived and built hotels, casinos, office towers, golf courses and other large scale projects; became a television star with *The Apprentice* TV series.

Fun Fact: Trump Tower was the shooting location for Wayne Enterprises in *The Dark Knight Rises*.

Write or Email the New President!

EMAIL: President@WhiteHouse.gov
Since 2014, the fastest way to contact the President is by email.

MAIL: President Trump
1600 Pennsylvania Avenue NW
Washington, DC 20500

Dear _____,

My name is _____and I am writing to tell you what I hope that you will accomplish as president:

1) _____

_____

_____

2) _____

_____

_____

3) _____

_____

_____

Sincerely,

_____(Your name)

Hail to the Chief

Picture yourself as the President. Fill in your name on the plaque.

President

Answers

Page 10
truths, equal, rights, life, liberty, happiness

Page 22
John Quincy Adams

Page 23
Calvin Coolidge

Page 26
Pauline

Page 27
Woodrow Wilson

Page 41
Lincoln

Page 49
Teddy

Page 52-53
F. Roosevelt, Kennedy, Reagan, T. Roosevelt, Adams

Page 57
Sarah Polk, Martha Washington, Eleanor Roosevelt, Dolley Madison, Abigail Fillmore

Page 58
Laura Bush, Lady Bird Johnson, Jackie Kennedy, Rosalynn Carter, Betty Ford

Page 67
Washington, Jefferson, Roosevelt, Lincoln

Page 71
39

Page 78
All of them

Made in the USA
Coppell, TX
29 July 2020